25

Stories with Moral for Kids Ages 7-9

EMAN
publishing

Cover Design by Madeeha Shaikh

Printed in the United States of America

Losers or Winners?

Sarah stared at the clock. It seemed like lunch was just not coming fast enough. Everything the teacher said came out as "blah, blah, blah." Her stomach rumbled. All

she could think about was the halal turkey sandwich her mom had made her. It was calling her from the coat room. She could practically taste it already!

Her teacher **glanced** at the clock as it finally ticked onto 11 o'clock. "Okay, kids, let's put away out things and get ready to head to the lunch room," she said.

"Finally," Sarah thought. "Lunch time!"

She and all of her classmates hurried into the coatroom to grab their lunches or lunch money. The elbow bumping and **jostling** of coats caused Sarah to be one of the last people in the coat room. She smiled when she saw her lunch. There was a turkey sandwich, an apple, a brownie, and pretzels waiting for her, and she couldn't wait. Taking a quick step to leave, she tripped on her untied shoelace. Maybe she could wait long enough to tie her shoe. She crouched down, and saw, peeking out from under the bench, a slightly crumpled five dollar bill. What a day! A great lunch, and she had found money on the floor. She tied her shoe and slipped the money into her pocket.

Smiling, she looked over, and saw her friend Nadia sitting on the bench, looking **frantically** through her book bag. Nadia was nearly in tears. Almost everything from her bag was on the floor in a scattered mess.

"What's wrong?" Sarah asked. "What are you looking for?"

Nadia looked up, startled. "I thought everyone had gone to lunch already. My mom gave me my lunch money this morning and I can't find it anywhere. I was supposed to bring her change. I can't eat lunch and I can't give my mom her change back. I don't know what to do." Tears started to well up in her eyes.

"How much did she give you?" Sarah asked, her happiness **deflating**.

"She gave me five dollars. I could have sworn I put it in my book bag, but it must have fallen out. You haven't seen it, have you?" Nadia asked, looking **forlorn**.

Sarah felt the money in her pocket burn. She knew it was Nadia's lunch money. She really wanted to keep it. She could go and buy a new necklace, or get some candy with it except the thought of lying to her friend made her stomach hurt. She couldn't do it.

"I think I found it under the bench when I was tying my shoe." Sarah said, reaching into her pocket. Handing Nadia the money, the knot in her stomach loosened up, and she smiled. It was good to know she had done the right thing. Nadia's face lit up like a candle and she jumped up and gave Sarah a hug.

"Thank you so much!" She exclaimed. "You made my day. Will you eat lunch with me?"

"I would love to," Sarah said, grinning

Narrated by Yazid:

The Prophet (*Salallahu alayhi was salam*) was asked about a Luqata (money found by somebody). He said: "Remember and recognize it's tying material and its container, and make public announcement about it for one year. If somebody comes and identifies it (then give it to him), otherwise add it to your property."

(Bukhari)

---

1. **Glanced:** to look quickly or briefly.
2. **Jostling**: to bump, push, shove, brush against, or elbow roughly or rudely.
3. **Frantically:** insane; mad.
4. **Deflating**: to release the air or gas from (something inflated, as a balloon).
5. **Forlorn:** unhappy or miserable.

Is cheating ok?

Today was a long day at school. Not only had there been one test, but two! Math and spelling, Sami's least favorites. Glad that the school day was over, Sami packed all his things into his book bag, ready to go home. His friend Adam rushed over to him, looking excited.

"Guess what!" Adam whispered. "I have a secret. Wanna know?"

"Well, maybe," Sami answered, unsure. "What kind of secret is it?"

Adam had a smirk on his face. "You know that spelling test we took today? Well, I had the word list written out on my hand. I'm going to get an A+!"

"That's cheating!" Sami exclaimed. "I don't know if that is the kind of secret I can keep."

Adam frowned. "Oh come on, everyone does it! It's not that big of a deal."

Sami looked at Adam and told him, "It's not fair for the people that took the test the way were supposed to. I didn't cheat. Besides, one of these days you will get caught, and get in really big trouble." Sami got up from his desk and started to leave the room. "It just isn't right to do things like that. Would your mom be proud of you?" He asked, hoping that Adam would say 'no'.

"No, I guess not." Muttered Adam as he looked at his feet, scuffing his shoe into the floor.

"I bet you'll be in less trouble if you tell the teacher now." said Sami, hoping that Adam would come clean.

"Tell Miss Martinez?! Are you kidding me? I'll fail. What good would that do?" Said Adam in an explosive whisper as he paced back and forth.

"Well, if you tell her you feel bad, she might let you take the test over, or give you another one." **conjectured** Sami.

Adam looked up from his feet. "Really? You think?"

"You won't know unless you ask." Sami told him, giving him a shove towards her desk.

Adam looked **desperately** back at him. He **appeared** to be ill.

Sami thought "It's a good thing there is a trash can by her desk,"

By the time Adam got to Miss Martinez's desk she was finished sorting papers. She looked up and smiled, but Adam didn't look any better. He muttered out what had happened, and she looked at him very seriously.

"Well Adam, it was a very good thing you did coming up to tell me what happened. It showed a lot of **integrity** to know that cheating is wrong. Now you know to not do it in the future, is that correct?" she asked him, very seriously.

Adam shook his head very fast, still looking like he was trying to not be sick.

"Good. I'm glad you won't be doing that again." she smiled at him. "But, about this test you took today. I can't count it. I'm going to have to throw it away. Because you came to me, I won't call your mother about this. But if it happens again, I will **immediately** pick up the phone. I will come up with something else for you to do, and it won't be as fun as a spelling test." Miss Martinez stood up and looked at Adam, and held out her hand. "Do we have a deal?"

"Yes m-a'am" he stuttered, shaking a little.

Sami came up and patted him on the back. "That wasn't so bad was it?"

"I g-guess not." said Adam still a little shaken. "I'm never ever doing that again. Ever- inshAllaah."

Narrated by 'Abdullah bin 'Umar:

A man mentioned to the Prophet that he had always been cheated in bargains. The Prophet (*Salallahu alayhi was salam*) said, "Whenever you do bargain, say, 'No cheating.'"

(Bukhari)

---

1. **Desperately:** having a great need for something.
2. **Appeared:** to look as if, to seem.
3. **Integrity:** to be honest and truthful.
4. **Immediately:** right away, to do something quickly without delay.

Helping a Friend!

Sitting with all her friends at lunch, Sarah and her friends saw a girl go by in **crutches**. She had a friend carrying her lunch, and she looked miserable. She had a cast on her leg, and she looked rather uncomfortable.

Amira had a sour look on her face. "Why does she have to eat in the lunch room, she is taking up so much room. I had to wait an extra five minutes just to get my lunch because she was in front of me." She **grumbled**, frowning at the girl. "She could at least let other people get past her so we don't have to wait for her to hobble around." Folding her arms, she glared at the girl, as if her look would make her go away.

There were mumbles of agreement from the other girls at the table. No one really liked having to doge her crutches, wait behind her, or hold the doors for her. It was just such a bother to have to do everything for her. It didn't seem fair.

Sarah glanced over at her, and she was picking at her lunch, her crutches on the floor. She looked like she had had better days. "Come on guys," Sarah said, "It's not like it happened on purpose. She didn't want to have her leg broken. Wouldn't you want people to help you if you had something like this happen to you? I know I would. Look at her, she looks like she is about to cry. It's not worth being mean to her, just because she has to use crutches."

Sarah got up, and looked at her friends. They were all very interested in their lunches. She shook her head and walked over to the girl. "Hello," She said. "My name is Sarah. I saw that you seemed sad. Are you ok?"

The girl looked up from her lunch. "Oh, yes, I'm fine. It's just been hard, with my leg. People don't seem to get it. I just feel it's in the way."

"That's awful! Well, if there is anything I can do to help; I'll be right over there." Sarah gave a small smile, and walked back over to her seat.

"Well, you guys, was that so hard? You act like there was something wrong with her. It's just a broken leg." She sat down and looked at her friends who didn't seem very proud of themselves. Nadia was **examining** her fingernails, Leena was inspecting her peas, and Amira appeared to be counting ceiling tiles.

"Hello? Anyone home?" Sarah asked, **frustrated.**

"Ok, ok." muttered Nadia. "I get it, we were mean."

Leena looked up from her peas and sighed. "I guess we shouldn't have been so harsh."

"Maybe if something like that happened to me, I would want people to help me, not be mad at me." Amira **reluctantly** decided.

Sarah looked at them and said, "I don't know about you, but I'm going to carry her books to class."

The bell rang signaling the end of lunch, and Amira went over to pick up her crutches off the ground. Nadia went over and took her tray to the trash, and Leena held the door.

For the first time that day, Sarah saw her smile. When Sarah grabbed her books, she whispered "Thank you," and slowly made her way to class.

Narrated by Abu Huraira:

The Prophet *(Salallahu alayhi was salam)* said, "Charity is obligatory everyday on every joint of a human being. If one helps a person in matters concerning his riding animal by helping him to ride it or by lifting his luggage on to it, all this will be regarded charity. A good word, and every step one takes to offer the compulsory Congregational prayer, is regarded as charity; and guiding somebody on the road is regarded as charity."

(Bukhari)

1. <u>**Crutches:**</u> a pole that helps injured people walk.
2. <u>**Grumbled:**</u> to complain, to moan.
3. <u>**Examining:**</u> looking carefully and closely at something.
4. <u>**Frustrated:**</u> feeling annoyed, cross or angry.
5. <u>**Reluctantly:**</u> not willing to do something.

It is Always Good to be Humble

This was the day! Their carpentry project was done. Jamal, Omar, Adam, and Sami, had built a bird house from scratch, painted it, and it was time to bring it to school. He had been **elected** by his friends to be the one to present it to the class.

Sitting in the car that morning with the bird house on his lap, he couldn't wait to get to school. He was nervous, excited, and ready to show everyone. It was a great thing to **behold,** the bird house. The top was green, the sides had spiders on them, the front had a sun around the opening, and the back had a moon. His dad had helped them use the hand saw and the hammers. He was so excited he could burst!

Pulling into the drive at school, his friends were waiting for him, and helped him out of the car. They all made sure the bird house made a safe **trek** into the classroom, and set it down on the table in the back of the room. The boys **anxiously** waited for the presentations to begin.

When their names were called, Sami's group stood up and he went to get the bird house from the table. He nervously brought it to the front of the class and looked at all his classmates. Knowing that they all soon had to give this same presentation, he took a deep breath and began to tell everyone about the bird house.

His friends stood behind him smiling and nodding, as he told the class about how Jamal was great at using the hammer, how Omar was excellent at using the saw, and how great Adam was at **designing** the roof. They had all taken turns painting and that the painting had been the best part.

When the presentation was done, he took it over to the windowsill, and smiled. He had done a good job. When class was over, some of his classmates came up to him telling him how excellent his bird house was and that his presentation was so good. He told them that the bird house never would have gotten done without his team.

"My friends did a lot of work on this bird house," Sami said. "Be sure to tell them what a good job you think they did too!" His classmates smiled and went over to the other members of his team. It felt good to make sure everyone got **acknowledged**.

Jamal came over and said, "Thanks for talking about us during the presentation that was really cool of you. Some people in the class didn't even get mentioned while their project was up."

Sami looked over at the bird house and said, "Without you guys there would be no bird house, so of course I had to talk about you guys!"

Adam was looking at the bird house and he said, "It was just nice to be thought of, so Jazak Allaah Khairan."

"Wyacum," Said Sami as he and his friends all

admired the bird house before going home.

The Prophet (*Salallahu alayhi was salam*) said:

"Keep yourselves far from envy; because it eats up and takes away good actions, like a fire eats up and burns wood."

(Abu Dawud)

---

1. **Elected:** choosing somebody by voting for them
2. **Behold:** to see or observe.
3. **Trek:** to go somewhere slowly, carefully or with difficulty.
4. **Anxiously:** feeling worried, uneasy and afraid of something.
5. **Acknowledged:** to show thanks or recognize someone's help or work.

Hard Work Pays Off....

Sarah was so sick of practicing. The bench was hard, and her bottom was sore. She knew she had a **recital** in a few weeks, but she was so sick of practicing. Didn't she deserve a break? It had been hours that she had been practicing,

hadn't it? She looked at the clock. Only 15 minutes?! No way. It had to have been longer than that. Her eyes were starting to go cross-eyed, and all the verses on the page just looked the same.

No, she couldn't quit now! No way. The surrah she had to recite for her recital was hard, and she wasn't very good at it yet. Shaking her head, hoping to clear away the fog, she looked back at the Qur'aan. "Bismillah she muttered.

This surrah was really hard. There were lots of tajweed rules, which meant, which meant her head had to do a lot of thinking. Her head would much rather be

thinking about playing outside with her friends. She realized she was staring at the wall, and not at the Qur'aan. In fact, her voice had stopped moving **entirely.**

"Bismillah..." she said, louder this time.

Trying to get through this surrah was like walking through snow a foot deep. "Hmmm." She thought, "Snow. **Sledding** would be awesome. Too bad it is August, and there isn't any snow."

Realizing she had drifted away again she stood up and walked around the room. This recital is important, and if she didn't practice, she would sound **ridiculous** in front of a lot of people, never mind Allaah swt.

Turning on her **speakers** she let it's steady click help guide her through the verses. With the speakers on, it was a lot harder for her to drift away. The sheikh recited so beautifully, mash'Allaah.

After finally having made progress, she looked up at the clock again. An hour had gone by! This was great! She really had gotten a lot of work done just because she had stuck with it and not given up. By the time the recital came, she would be able to recite this surah like a pro!

"Well," she thought, "It couldn't hurt to go through it just one more time."

"Bismillah..." She said, and this time began reciting herself.

Narrated by Abu Huraira:

The Prophet (*Salallahu alayhi was salam*) said,
"Religion is very easy and whoever overburdens
himself in his religion will not be able to continue in
that way. So you should not be extremists, but try to be
near to perfection and receive the good tidings that you
will be rewarded; and gain strength by worshipping in
the mornings, the nights."

(Bukhari)

---

1. **Recital:** reading out loud from memory.
2. **Entirely:** completely, altogether.
3. **Sledding:** a flat piece of wood used to travel on snow or ice.
4. **Ridiculous:** completely silly and funny.
5. **Speakers:** an electronic equipment that gives out sound.

The Science Project

The science fair was tomorrow, and Sarah was excited. She had made the coolest volcano and it worked so well. She couldn't wait to go to school and show it off. Putting the finishing touches on the paint, she stepped back and looked at it. It was great. She had the presentation all ready about what volcanoes were and how they were formed. She had found pictures of active volcanoes,  and pictures of some of the most deadly volcanoes in history. Washing her hands and paint brushes, she got ready to go to bed.

* * *

The next morning, Sarah took her project to school and set it up in the auditorium. All her classmates were setting up their projects. Nadia's project was on the growth cycle of butterflies. Amira did her project on the solar system. Everyone in her class was hoping to get the blue ribbon. It was **gigantic**, it's length being at about one foot long. There were projects on tadpoles, the moon, the ocean, growing flowers, and so many more. Sarah hoped she did well, but it would be ok if someone else won. Everyone had worked just as hard as she had.

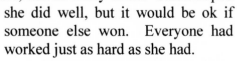

Teachers were **milling** around the **auditorium** with clipboards, parents were looking at all the different projects, and everyone was waiting for the teachers to get to them so that they could present their project.

A teacher she didn't know came up to Sarah, and asked her about her project. She took notes on the clipboard and smiled. "Thank you, have a good after noon." Sarah told the teacher as she walked away. She was nervous now.

She had her project looked at by a teacher, and now all she could do was show it to the people that came by and asked questions. But first, she had 'lava' to clean up. Baking soda and vinegar bubbles make quite a mess.

After what seemed like an age, they asked everyone to take as seat, as they were going to announce the winners. The principal came up to the microphone.

"Thank you all for **participating** today! You all worked so hard, and did such great work. I'm proud of all of you. It's time to announce the winners for this year's Science Fair!" The principal looked out at everyone with a big grin. He looked down at the clipboard he was holding and began to announce honorable mentions. There were 5 of them. All of them went up to the front and took their ribbons.

"Now for 3rd place!" He said, looking back at his clipboard. Again, he announced the name of a boy Sarah didn't know. She was beginning to feel **downhearted**. She couldn't possibly have done better than 3rd place! Everyone had done so well, and on top of that, there had been someone else that had a volcano.

He announced 2nd place with no **avail**. Sarah was about to give up and looked at the floor, when all of a sudden, people were cheering and patting her on the back.

Nadia looked at her and said "You won!"

She looked up and saw that people were looking at her. She stood up, dazed and walked up towards the front. The principal smiled at her and shook her hand, and congratulated her. People where clapping and patting her on the back. She didn't know what to do, other than just smile, and tell everyone else that they did just as good a job as she did. It's easier for her to tell others that they did a good job than to accept all of the praise she was getting for winning.

Prophet Muhammad (*Salallahu alayhi was salam*) said:

"The affair of the believer is amazing! The whole of his life is beneficial, and that is only in the case of the believer. When good times come to him, he is thankful and it is good for him, and when bad time...s befall him, he is patient and it is also good for him"

(Muslim)

---

1. **Gigantic**: very large, huge, and enormous.
2. **Milling:**
3. **Auditorium:** a large room or building where people gather for a performance or speech.
4. **Participating:** to take part is something.
5. **Downhearted:** sad, unhappy, low.
6. **Avail:** to be useful, to have an advantage.

The Bracelet

During break time, Sarah and her friends were sitting out on a bench. Sarah was reading a book, and not **particularly** paying attention to what was going on. Hearing **commotion**, she looked up, puzzled.

"I found it first!" Nadia snapped at Amira, with a bitter look on her face. "It was by my foot!"

Amira had hold of one end of a bracelet, and Nadia had a firm grip on the other end. "You did not find it first! And my foot is right next to yours!" Amira said, her voice rising. "Finders-keepers!"

"Well that would be great if *you* had found it first, but I did, so it's mine!" Nadia said, nearly shouting now.

Sarah looked at them both, shocked. This wasn't like them. It was just a dumb bracelet.

"Guys!" Sarah **interrupted**. "What are you doing? Fighting over a bracelet that isn't even yours? What's gotten in to you?"

Nadia looked over at her surprised. "But I found it..." she muttered.

"Who cares who found it?" Sarah said. "It doesn't belong to either one of you. Someone lost it, and is

probably looking for it, and you are bickering over who is going to keep it. How is that fair to the person that lost it?"

Amira blushed and let go of the bracelet. "I guess I never thought of that." She frowned and looked at her shoes. Nadia looked at the bracelet in her hand. It was one that had been woven and was full of color. Someone ad spent a lot of time on it. "Do you think that we can find out who it belongs to?" She said **inquisitively**.

"Well," Sarah said. "The only way to find out is to turn it in to our teacher and say we found it out by the bench. Maybe someone has asked for it."

Getting up, the girls found their way across the playground to their teacher.

"Miss Farzana," said Nadia. "We found this by the bench and were wondering if anyone had lost it."

"That is very considerate of you girls," Miss Farzana said. "No one has come up to me yet, but I'll hold on to it in case they do. Jazak Allaah Khairan." Their teacher smiled and took the bracelet and put it in her pocket.

"I suppose that was the right thing to do," said Amira, a bit glum.

"Well, it looked like someone made that bracelet, so maybe we can learn how to make them ourselves? I think that would be better than taking one off the ground that belongs to someone else." Sarah **suggested**.

Nadia and Amira looked at each other and smiled. "That sounds great! Maybe a sleep over?"

"Totally!" said Sarah. They all walked away happy, knowing that the right thing had been done.

Narrated by Yazid:

The Prophet *(Salallahu alayhi was salam)* was asked about a Luqata (money found by somebody). He said, "Remember and recognize it's tying material and its container, and make public announcement about it for one year. If somebody comes and identifies it (then give it to him), otherwise add it to your property."

(Bukhari)

---

1. <u>**Particularly:**</u> specifically, to do something with great attention to detail.
2. <u>**Commotion:**</u> a noisy confusion or activity.
3. <u>**Interrupted:**</u> to speak over or in the middle of someone.
4. <u>**Inquisitively:**</u> curiously, eager to know or learn.
5. <u>**Suggested:**</u> to give an idea, to put forth your own view.

The Bully

Lunch was beginning to be an unpleasant place to go to. Every day it seemed that their class bully was going to do something else to make everyone's lives miserable. Latifa was bigger than most of the girls in the class and she was meaner too. No one was quite sure why, but she had a thing for stealing peoples lunches. **Unfortunately**, today, Amira had been picked.

"Hand it over, NOW!" Latifa shouted, reaching over and trying to grab Amira's brown bag.

"Leave me alone!" Amira **pleaded**, holding her lunch bag close to her chest and trying to dodge the bullies grasps.

"I want that lunch! Give it over!" Latifa demanded, her hands making **unfruitful** swipes at Amira's chest.

"Get your own lunch!" Amira squeaked, ducking another grab.

"What do you think I'm doing loser! I'm getting my lunch! Now hand it over before this gets rough!" Latifa threatened, starting to make a grab for Amira's hair.

Sarah had just walked into the lunch room. There was a small group of people starting to crowd around the table to watch the **altercation.** As she got closer, she heard her friends voice, desperate and scared.

"Just hand it over and all this will stop," Latifa growled.

Sarah had heard enough. She had seen a dozen people have their lunches stolen, and Latifa wave them around like trophies. Now one of her best friends was caught up in this. It was too much.

"STOP IT!" She shouted over the noise of the chattering group, Latifa, and Amira's pleading.   Latifa looked at her **disbelievingly.** The group that had gathered all looked at her too. Amira quickly got up from the lunch table and got behind her.

"What are you going to do about it?" Latifa **jeered**.

"I'm going to ask you to just leave people alone. If you need lunch, ask a teacher or something. Stop taking it from people."   Sarah said, glaring. "Scaring people isn't making people like you."

Latifa stood there, staring at her. "Fine, pipsqueak. Today, your scared little friend can have her little lunch, but I wouldn't bet on tomorrow, or the next day."

She jumped down from the table she was sitting on and stormed out of the lunch room.

"Are you ok?" Sarah asked Amira, looking back at her.

"Yeah, I'm ok. My lunch is a little squished, but other than that, I'm fine. Do you really think she will come back tomorrow to try to take it again?" Amira asked, a bit shakily.

"Who knows," Sarah said. "What I do know is that it was time that someone stood up to her. What she was doing was wrong."

"What you did was brave," said Nadia as she walked over.

"Brave, maybe. I just hope it she won't come back- inshAllaah." Said Sarah, looking out the door Latifa had just stormed out of.

Narrated by 'Abdullah bin 'Amr:

The Prophet (*Salallahu alayhi was salam*) said, "Whoever has the following four (characteristics) will be a pure hypocrite and whoever has one of the following four characteristics will have one characteristic of hypocrisy unless and until he gives it up. 1. Whenever he is entrusted, he betrays. 2. Whenever he speaks, he tells a lie. 3. Whenever he makes a covenant, he proves treacherous. 4. Whenever he quarrels, he behaves in a very imprudent, evil and insulting manner."

(Bukhari)

---

1. **Unfortunately:** used when somebody wishes something were not true.
2. **Pleaded:** to ask in a honest or serious way
3. **Unfruitful:**
4. **Altercation:** argument, quarrel, fight
5. **Disbelievingly:** to refuse to believe in, to think that it is untrue.
6. **Jeered:** to shout or laugh at someone in a mocking or rude way.

Giving is Better than Receiving

"Knock-Knock!" Sarah heard someone at her bedroom door. It was Saturday, and it was way too early. "Good morning, Sunshine!" said her mom, as she opened the door.

"Can I just get up tomorrow?" Sarah moaned as she rolled over and put a pillow on her face.

"No way, habibti! We have something important to do today!" Her mom beamed at her as she pulled the blankets and pillows off and reached down to tickle her. Giggling, Sarah got up and wiped the sleep out of her eyes. "Breakfast first, then we will get down to business." Her mom **herded** her down the stairs where her brother was already sitting with sleepy eyes staring at a plate of pancakes.

"Now today, we are going through all of your toys and clothes and finding the things that don't fit, or that you don't wear, the toys that you have out grown and you don't play with anymore, and we are going to donate them to people that aren't as **fortunate** as we are."

"But I like my toys," Sami muttered stabbing at a pancake.

"I don't have any clothes or toys I want to give

away!" Sarah exclaimed, alarmed at the thought.

"Now kids," said Mom, "I know for a fact that there are toys in your rooms you haven't played with since you were at least 3 years old. What do you need them for? And what in the world do you need to keep shirts and pants that you out grew last year for? There are people that can't afford to buy nice new clothes and toys like you have. It's time to clean out your toy boxes, closets and dressers. No more discussion."

Sarah and Sami **trudged** up the stairs and went into their rooms. Sarah looked at all of her things. She had shirts and pants and sweaters and socks and shoes and stuffed animals that she hadn't done a thing with in a long time. It wasn't so much that, but the fact that they were hers. Going to the closet she picked up a pair of pants she'd had since she was 4. They were so small. Those had to go, even if they were purple.

 It took a long time to go through everything, but in the end she had a small mountain of clothes, and a larger mountain of toys that she knew she wasn't going to need again. Her mom had come in to check on the **progress**, and had told her that she was very proud of her. There were some little girls that were going to love these things, and that it very **generous** of her to go through all of her things and find so much to give away.

Narrated by Abu Huraira:

A man asked the Prophet (*Salallahu alayhi was salam*), "O Allaah's Apostle! What kind of charity is the best?" He replied. "to give in charity when you are healthy and greedy hoping to be wealthy and afraid of becoming poor. Don't delay giving in charity till the time when you are on the death bed when you say, 'Give so much to so-and-so and so much to so-and so,' and at that time the property is not yours but it belongs to so-and-so (i.e. your inheritors)."

(Bukhari)

---

1. **Herded:** to move people or animals somewhere as a group or to collect them into one .
2. **Fortunate:** to be lucky and blessed.
3. **Trudged:** to walk with slow, heavy, tired steps.
4. **Progress:** to move forwards towards an aim.
5. **Generous:** kind, willing to give, not be selfish.

Getting Cold Teeth

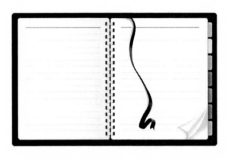

This book report was **awful**. Simply awful. It made Sarah want to run and hide in a corner and never come out. She had to present this report in front of the entire class. It wasn't that she didn't like the book. That wasn't it at all. The book had been a joy to read, but the idea of having to tell everyone in the class everything she had liked about it, wasn't fun at all. Could it just be that she wasn't made out to be a public speaker? That had to be it. She was meant to be a clam. They just hid away in their shells, not bothering anyone. They didn't have to get up in front of people and talk for 5 minutes. Goodness, those 5 minutes might as well be 5 years. No, 10 years. By the time she would be done giving this report she would be ready to get her driver's license and she would be able to just drive away into the sunset.

She banged her head down on her desk. This couldn't be worse. It really couldn't. The only way it could be worse was if she had to do it without a hijab. Luckily, that wasn't the case. She **sighed** deeply and looked around her room. Was there any way to make this better? Any way at all? There was a knock at her door.

"Who is it?" She said, and sighed again.

"Just Dad, coming to check in on that book report," he said with a smile.

"It's just awful, terrible, and more awful," Sarah told him, putting her head in her hands. "I just can't get up in front of those people."

"Well sure you can! You are a lot better at it than you think. Do you ever raise your hand in class?" He asked as he walked over to her bed.

"Of course I do! What does that have to do with anything?" Sarah looked at him, **puzzled**.

"Well, the whole class hears you when you get called on then, don't they?  This isn't that much different. Your classmates already know what you look like, so standing in front of them isn't that bad, and they know what you sound like because you answer questions in class. So, basically, you are being called on to tell about your book. Does that help?" He looked her way and smiled.

"It actually does. I have a lot less to be afraid of than I thought, Alhamdullilah! Thanks dad." She went over and gave him a hug. "Do you want to hear my report?"

"Sure thing kiddo. And if you get nervous, just think of you alone, and you'll be fine." They both laughed, and Sarah began her report with a smile.

The Prophet Musa (may Allaah grant him peace), after being commissioned by Allaah to go to Pharaoh (Fir'aun), said to Allaah:

"O my Lord! Open for me my chest (grant me self-confidence, contentment, and boldness). And ease my task for me; and make loose the knot (the defect) from my tongue, that they may understand my speech."

(The Qur'an, Chapter 20:25-28)

---

1. **Awful:** very bad, terrible, poor.
2. **Sighed:** to breathe out with a long breath because of being sad, tired, or relieved.
3. **Puzzled:** being confused, something that is hard to understand.

Patience with Siblings

It was the perfect day to read a book. There was a breeze coming in through the window, the skies were blue, and all of Sarah's homework was done. Taking in a deep breath of the fresh air, she grabbed a book from her shelf and laid down on her bed. What a perfect start to an afternoon.

About a half an hour had passed when she heard a noise. "sshhhh-thump" Looking out of her bedroom door, and seeing nothing, she shook it off and went back to her book. Then it came. A Nerf ball to the leg.

"Sami!!" She called out. "Quit it! I want to read!" Shaking her head and going back to her book, she tried to ignore her brother. He wasn't going to be allowed to ruin her day. Not a chance!

"Sssssshhhhh-poomph!" This time the ball hit her book. It fell onto her face and she lost her page.

"Hey! That hurt! What do you think you are doing?" She shouted out after him. Putting her book on the bed, she got up and looked into the hallway. He was gone. "Brothers," she muttered. Going back to her book, she **rifled** through the pages trying to find her place.

This time she didn't lay down. Keeping one eye on the door and one eye on her book, she waited. She knew Sami was going to try it again. She just knew it. He had to be creeping around in the hallway somewhere. She was **intently** listening for his footsteps, or the clank of the ball launcher. Anything that might give him away. Finally she heard him. The soft sound of padded feet on the floor. She pretended to not hear a thing. Looking out of the corner of her eye, she saw him in the doorway and sprang up.

"Ahh-Ha!" She shouted! "I caught you in the act!" He dropped the ball he was going to throw and looked **sheepish**.

"I was just having some fun," Sami said, crossing his arms.

"And I was trying to read my book. I would appreciate it if you could shoot these at someone else. I don't want to have to kick you out of my room." Sarah said picking the balls up from the floor and handing them back. "Can you do target practice in the backyard or something?"

"Yeah, I guess so. I didn't mean to have your book land on your face. I was aiming for the headboard and it went low. Sorry." Sami took his ammunition from Sarah, and started to leave.

"It's ok," she told him. "Just don't aim for me in general, please."

"Yes ma'am," he said giving her a **sarcastic** salute.

Once she was sure he had gone outside and was shooting things like the fence, she laid back down and reached for her book. "Who knows what brothers are for," she thought. "But at least they make life interesting."

Jubayr ibn Nufayr reported that Mu'adh ibn Jabal said:

"If you love someone, do not quarrel with him and do not annoy him. Do not ask others about him, for the one you ask might be his enemy and thus tell you things about him that are not true and thus break you apart."

(Bukhari)

---

1. **Rifled:** to search through something.
2. **Intently:** closely, carefully, with full attention.
3. **Sheepish:** being embarrassed when you have done something foolish.
4. **Sarcastic:** using words that are meant to hurt or make fun of another person.

Tough Decision

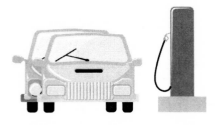

They had been in the car, running **errands** for hours. Sarah was hot, her behind hurt, and she just wanted to go home. "One last stop guys, I need to go into the bookstore and get a book for work. I might even let you get something because you have been so good today on all these errands." Dad looked into the rear view mirror and smiled back at the two of them. Sami wasn't paying attention, but Sarah was. Sarah loved the bookstore. There were so many new books, the smell of coffee, newspapers, and the general atmosphere was just thrilling to Sarah. It made an achy bottom totally worth the wait.

Getting in to the bookstore, her dad told them that they could both pick out one book to bring home. Sami wandered away, heading towards books on nature. Sarah didn't know where to go. This place was huge. There were books on every topic. From the history of the World, to huge books called coffee table books. This was going to be a hard choice.

She wandered over to the children's section and saw row after row of chapter books. There were mysteries, stories about horses, aliens, you name it, someone had written about it. She wandered over to the books about horses. There were at least four different series that had to do with horses.

"This just isn't fair," she muttered under her breath.

Picking up the four of them, she sat down on the ground, right in front of the shelf. She looked at the four books on her lap. Knowing she could only pick one, she started reading the blurb that was on the back of each one. One was about girls at a ranch, one was about girls learning how to ride, the other was about a family that owned a ranch and took care of horses for others. The last was about a girl that got lost in the woods with only her pack and her horse.

Reading the back didn't make it any easier. She let out a sigh. Maybe the one about the ranch? No, too **generic**. How about the one with the family that owned the ranch? No, that's too close to the other one. That left the other two. She laid the other books aside and looked at the two left. On one there was a picture of four girls **gleefully** riding horses, looking like the world was complete. The other book had a picture of a girl that looked like she had been rained on, her clothes were dirty, and she was  leading her horse by its **reins** through what looked like a clearing in a forest. She wondered what it would be like to be stuck all alone in the forest with a horse. This is it; she had made up her mind.

Putting the other books back where she found them, she went to get her dad. She was proud that she had made a **decision**, even if it had been a tough one. She couldn't wait to read this book. It looked like quite an adventure.

Narrated Ibn Masud: I heard the Prophet saying *(Salallahu alayhi was salam)*:

"There is no envy except in two: a person whom Allah has given wealth and he spends it in the right way, and a person whom Allaah has given wisdom (i.e. religious knowledge) and he gives his decisions accordingly and teaches it to the others."

(Bukhari)

---

1. **Errands:** a short trip taken for a particular reason.
2. **Generic:** general, broad or basic.
3. **Gleefully:** happily, cheerfully.
4. **Reins:** leather straps used to control the horse.
5. **Decision:** the act of making your mind up.

A Sad Day

Leena came to school one morning with puffy eyes and a sadness about her. She came into the coat room and slowly hung her coat up. Sniffing, she put her book bag on the floor.

"Leena, what's wrong?" Nadia asked, coming over to her.

Sarah went to her and put her hand on her shoulder. "Are you ok?" she asked.

Sniffling, Leena looked up at her friends. "My cat, Scribbles, ran out into the street last night and got hit by a car." She **sniveled** and kept going. "He was my best friend, and such a good cat. I- I'm going to m-miss him!" With that she began to cry in **earnest** and put her head in her hands. Her small shoulders shook with sobs as she wept. "I'll never e-ever have a cat as good as him!"

Sarah sat down on the bench next to her and put her arm over Leena's shoulders. It was awful to lose a pet. She should know, they had had a cat die not too long ago.

"*Inna lilhe wi inna lillahe rajoon. (To Allaah we belong and to Allaah we return)* I know it's hard now, and it's ok to miss him. I miss Whiskers, my kitty. He was sick and he had to be put to sleep. My dad told me that he isn't in pain anymore and that he wouldn't want me to be sad all the time. To try and remember all the fun we had together." Sarah told Leena gently.

Leena **sniffed** and tried wiping away some of the tears with her sleeve. "Y-yeah. We did have a lot of fun together. He loved to play with the yarn ball. He was really good at it. And my daddy and I took him out with us to the park all the time. Scribbles loved to run and touch everything. He was a happy cat. He wouldn't want me to cry."

Sarah smiled. "It's ok to cry a little, but he would want you to be happy. It'll be ok Leena. Don't worry."

"Thanks Sarah, I feel a whole lot better." Lenna wiped the rest of her tears away.

"Jazak Allaah Khairan," Sarah said, helping Lenna grab her books.

The two of them went into class, both of them thinking fondly of their pets, knowing that it was ok to miss them and think about them.

Narrated by 'Abdullah bin 'Umar :

Sad bin 'Ubada became sick and the Prophet (*Salallahu alayhi was salam*) along with 'Abdur Rahman bin 'Auf, Sad bin Abi Waqqas and 'Abdullah bin Masud visited him to enquire about his health. When he came to him, he found him surrounded by his household and he asked, "Has he died?" they said, "No, O Allaah's Apostle." the Prophet wept and when the people saw the weeping of Allaah's Apostle (p.b.u.h) they all wept. He said, "Will you listen? Allaah does not punish for shedding tears, nor for the grief of the heart but he punishes or bestows His Mercy because of this." He pointed to his tongue and added, "the deceased is punished for the wailing of his relatives over him." 'Umar used to beat with a stick and throw stones and put dust over the faces (of those who used to wail over the dead).

(Bukhari)

---

1. **Sniveled:** to weep or cry whilst sniffling.
2. **Earnest:** done in a honest and sincere way.
3. **Sniffed:** to take in short breaths of air through the nose that can be heard.

Always Keep the End in Mind

This math test is 35% of Sarah's grade in Math.

She had study guides, a practice test, and everything she needed to prepare for it. The only problem was the fact that her friend, Amira was having her Eid party the night before the test. The party was on a Sunday and the test was on a Monday morning. Her mom had told her that she could go to the party, but only if she had studied for the test first. It was so unfair that they had to be so close together. She let out a big sigh. There wasn't anything she could do about it. Amira had to have the party that day because it was the only day her family from out of state could be there. Amira's mom was making her study before the party too, and it was her Eid.

Sarah didn't really like math, but she did like cake. "Hmm," Sarah wondered. "Maybe if I think of each problem I work on as a step closer to eating the cake! That might do the trick." Sitting down at her desk she began to think of cake and math. You

needed math to make cake. If you didn't have the correct **measurements** of the right things, it wouldn't be a cake. Just like if the math problem didn't have all the correct

"Yeah, it really did. I kept **pondering** about all the cake I would miss out on if I didn't do well on the practice test, and that made it a lot easier to study." Sarah said with a laugh.

"Cake is always a good motivator, I'm just glad you got your work done." Her mom said.

"Me too," Sarah said. "So about that Eid present, ready to go inshAllaah?"

Dua for Laziness:

O Allah! I seek refuge in You from anxiety and sorrow, weakness and laziness, miserliness and cowardice, the burden of debts and from being oppressed by men.

1. <u>**Measurements:**</u> the specific size of something that has been measured.
2. <u>**Motivation:**</u> the desire to act because of a reason.
3. <u>**Pondering:**</u> to think carefully and deeply about something.

Borrowing from a Friend

After school one afternoon, Nadia and Sarah were talking in the parking lot waiting for their parents to pick them up from school. Nadia had brought with her a bracelet to **borrow**, and was telling her all about it.

"My grandmother gave this to me, so you have to be super **attentive**," Nadia told Sarah as she opened the box. It was a silver bracelet that had a single heart hanging from it. It **sparkled** in the afternoon sun. "Please be careful with it, I really like it a lot, and it's the only thing I have that is like it."

"I will be very careful with it I promise. It won't come out of the box until right before the recital, I promise!" Sarah said, taking the box and carefully putting it in her book bag.

Coming home, all Sarah could think about was that bracelet. It would be the perfect thing to wear during her Qur'aan recital, and she couldn't wait to put it on. She was so excited, that she could burst! She also knew that it was a big responsibility to wear her friend's bracelet. If anything happened to it, she would be **devastated**.

Rushing up the stairs, she pulled out the dress she was going to wear. It was blue with white ribbon around the middle. The silver bracelet would look wonderful while she recited her Qur'aan. She quickly got dressed, and her mom came in to help her fix her hijab. The very last thing she did was go to her book bag and get the box out of it. Opening the box, there lay the silver bracelet. It caught light and just sparkled. It would be perfect. Her mom put it on for her, and they readied themselves to go to the recital.

* * *

The next morning at school, Sarah beamed and handed the box and bracelet back to Nadia. "Thank you so very much for letting me borrow it! It was just what I needed for the recital." She said.

Nadia took the bracelet back, and smiled. "It wasn't a big deal. I knew you would take great care of it. I bet it looked great while you were reciting!"

"Oh, it did! My mom told me it glittered in the light. It was perfect!" Sarah exclaimed.

"Well, be sure to let me know when your next recital is, you can borrow it then too," said Nadia, putting the bracelet away.

"Thanks, Nadia, I'll be sure to let you know. Maybe next time you can come and see how it looks yourself!" Sarah said, just as the first bell rang for class.

The Prophet (*Salallahu alayhi was salam*):

"Kindness is a mark of faith, and whoever is not kind has no faith."

(Muslim)

---

1. **Borrow:** to take with the promise of giving it back.
2. **Attentive:** paying close attention, careful.
3. **Sparkled:** shine, glitter, shimmer.
4. **Devastated:** to be extremely upset .

Don't Judge Food, Try It!

Sarah and Leena were very excited for that night. They were finally going to have dinner at Leena's house. They had so many things planned. From watching a movie, to **braiding** each other's hair, to making bracelets, their night was packed. Before they could do everything they had planned, they had to eat. Leena had been begging for pizza all week, but her mom said no. She was **pouting** and rather **disappointed**.

"But Moooom! My friend is here and I want pizza! It's not fair! Chicken is soo booreing!" Leena whined.

"Chicken is not booooreing, and that's that." Her mother admonished, leaving Leena standing in the kitchen to pout.

"I don't mind chicken Mrs. Hashim it's really not a big deal." Sarah said, trying to be helpful.

Leena frowned, and said, "Yeah, but you've never had my mom's chicken. It's lame."

Sarah shrugged. "It can't be that bad. Maybe we can have pizza the next time, right Mrs. Hashim?"

"Maybe next time. And my chicken isn't 'lame'. I promise. Leena is just being a sick in the mud. Why don't you two go wash up. Dinner will be ready soon." Mrs. Hashim said, getting plates down from the cupboard.

"I hate chicken." Leena pouted. "I never want to eat it again," she muttered as the girls washed their hands.

"You don't hate chicken. Chicken nugget day is your favorite lunch at school." Sarah pointed out, drying her hands off.

"Well, it's not better than pizza, and there is nothing you can say about that." Leena snapped as she left the bathroom.

Heading towards the kitchen, the girls found dinner laid out on the table. Sarah thought it smelled great, but Leena was **determined** to fuss about it.

"Wow! Dinner smells great. Thanks for making it Mrs. Hashim," Sarah said, taking her seat.

Leena slid into her chair glowering at the roasted chicken

on the table. She looked about ready to throw it across the dining room and into the hall. At this rate, maybe she would.

"Thank you, Sarah, I hope you enjoy it," Leena's mother said serving her some food. She did the same for Leena, but Leena didn't move. She looked at it like she didn't know what to do with it.

Sarah leaned over and whispered "Just eat your dinner, your mom worked hard on it, and it just isn't right to not eat it like that."

Leena sighed, sat up and grabbed her fork. She poked at the chicken, still not taking a bite. She looked over at Sarah, **incredulously.** Sarah gave a little nod, and she started to eat. It must not have been so bad after all. She ate all that was on her plate, and dessert. She wished she had not been so mean to her mom. "I am sorry mom, your chicken is good," Said Leena. "It's ok, honey, I am glad that you like it," said her mom.

Mu'adh (May Allah be pleased with him) reported:

The Messenger of Allah (*Salallahu alayhi was salam*) took hold of my hand and said:

"O Mu'adh! By Allah I love you, so I advise you to never forget to recite after every prayer:

Allahumma a'inni alaa dhikrika, wa shukrika, wa husni 'ibaadatika

(O Allaah, help me remember You, to be grateful to You, and to worship You in an excellent manner)."

(Abu Dawud)

---

1. **Braiding:** to weave together three or more strands of hair to form one length that looks like a rope.
2. **Pouting:** to show unhappy feelings with an expression of the face .
3. **Disappointed:** let down, upset, something was not as expected.
4. **Determined:** the quality of having a firm goal, not giving up.
5. **Incredulously:** unable or unwilling to believe something.

Chores, Chores and Chores!

It was another early Saturday morning. The birds were happy about it, but Sarah wished they hadn't woken her up at 7 o'clock. This Saturday was all about chores, chores, chores. Today she had to help her mom with the laundry. Her mom put everything in the washer, and it was her job to take everything out when it was dry and do all the folding. There was a ton of laundry to do today because they had to change all the sheets on all the beds. That was a whole lot folding. Not to mention they had come back from vacation not too long ago and the laundry was still piled up after that.

With a groan, Sarah put her feet on the floor. She shivered. It was cold. She shuffled over to her dresser and grabbed a pair of socks. It was time to get going.

Finding her mom in the kitchen, she knew that the big laundry day had already started. She could smell the fabric softener **wafting** up from the basement. There were four **amply** sized baskets of dirty clothes waiting to go downstairs for when her dad woke up. That mountain was just clothes! The bed sheets were still on the beds of the sleeping people.

She got down a bowl for cereal and began to eat, listening for the driers buzzer to go off. It couldn't be too long now. She let out a big yawn. This was going to be a long day. "Bzzzzzzzzzzt!"

There is was. Time to go. She picked up her feet

and shuffled her way drowsily into the basement. Pulling the dry clothes out of the drier she piled them into a large basket. Grabbing hold of its handles, she pulled it to the stairs and it clunked its way up the stairs along with her. Moving into the living room, she began to fold socks, shirts, towels, and pants. She even had to fold her brothers underwear. Ewww. This baskets folding was finished, and she knew that her mom had put another load in the drier because she could hear it's gentle hum.

"Hey mom, how much longer on that load?" Sarah called out.

"About 25 minutes or so," she heard her mom calling back to her from some distant place in the house.

Sarah let out another yawn and laid her head down on the clean clothes she had just folded. They were still warm, and smelled nice. It would only be for a second.

"Bzzzzzzzzzzt!"

Sarah was startled awake. The timer on the drier had gone off again. It was a shame she was so warm and cozy. Maybe a few more minutes. No. That was a bad idea. **Dozing** off on the job. It was time for the next load to be done. At least this chore smelled good. Her brother was outside with Dad learning how to clean the **gutters**. Folding laundry was better any day.

She yawned and got up, and started the **cycle** all over again. This time, without the nap.

Narrated by Al-Miqdam:

The Prophet *(Salallahu alayhi was salam)* said,
"Nobody has ever eaten a better meal than that which
one has earned by working with one's own hands. The
Prophet of Allah, David used to eat from the earnings
of his manual labor."

(Bukhari)

1. **Wafting:** floating gently through the air.
2. **Amply:** fully, more than enough.
3. **Dozing:** to sleep lightly for a short time.
4. **Gutters:** a pipe under the lower edge of a roof for
   carrying off water.

Generous Friends

Leena was sitting at the lunch table, with her hands in her lap. It had just been a **rotten** day. Completely awful. She had been late to school and she had forgotten

her lunch. She had just heard her stomach **rumble**. "Wonderful," she thought. "I can't do anything about it either."

Sarah, Nadia, and Amira all joined her at the table. Sarah noticed she wasn't eating, and was staring at her lap. "What's wrong?" Sarah asked. "Why aren't you eating lunch?"

Leena looked up, having just noticed that her friends had sat down around her. "Oh, I forgot my lunch. It was a rough morning."

"What happened?" Nadia asked dumping her lunch bag out on the table.

Leena frowned and looked back down at her hands. "Our cat got out into the backyard. She is a house cat, so my dad spent almost a half an hour trying to catch her. By the time he did, I was late for school, and I **managed** to leave my lunch in the refrigerator."

Amira dumped her lunch out, and Sarah did the same. Normally at lunch they **swapped** parts of their lunches around for things they wanted better. Today, Sarah had an idea.

"Hey, how about we go through our lunches, like usual, only we share with Leena. That way she has a lunch today." She suggested.

The other two looked at each other, shrugged and nodded. Leena looked up and smiled.

"You would do that for me?" she asked, a little **dumfounded.**

"Sure thing!" Sarah said, breaking her sandwich in half. "It is what friends do for one another."

Nadia gave Leena her chips, and Amira gave her some fruit snacks.

"You guys are the best!" said Leena, taking a bite of the sandwich.

"None of my friends should have to go hungry at lunch time!" Sarah told her, eating the other half of the sandwich. "Though, I am glad your dad found your cat."

Leena smiled nodded. "Me too. She freaks out when she gets outside. The neighbor's dog scares her. Though, I really wish she could have picked a better time to get out than right before school." She shrugged her shoulders and looked down at the lunch her friends had given her. "Really appreciate the food guys. It means a lot." she said, **sheepishly**.

"Not a problem," said Sarah.

"Sure thing," Amira replied.

"Any time," said Nadia.

Narrated by Ibn 'Umar:

The Prophet *(Salallahu alayhi was salam)* decreed that one should not eat two dates together at a time unless he gets the permission from his companions (sharing the meal with him).

(Bukhari)

1. **Rotten:** bad, awful, terrible .
2. **Rumble:** to make a long, low, rolling sound.
3. **Managed:** get along, able to, cope, make do.
4. **Swapped:** change, switch, trade.
5. **Dumfounded:** to confuse, amaze or astonish someone.
6. **Sheepishly:** awkwardly, with embarrassment.

Eid Party!

The twins Eid party was coming up fast, and man were they ready. Sami was excited about the pool party; Sarah was excited about the **decorations**. Their mom had been planning this party for weeks. It was going to be awesome. All their friends at school were talking about it, and no one could wait!

The day of the party, they were busy setting up tables, getting the banner set up, and putting all of the stuff in the goodie bags so that they were packed and ready to go. It was an awesome day for a pool party. The sun was out and had lots of bright white clouds to go with it.

The only thing that could make Sarah more excited would be the big chocolate cake that was coming to the house soon. She and her brother didn't get along when it came to a lot of things, but when it came to cake, chocolate was the best. They had gone to a bakery with their mom and gotten to choose how the cake would look, what kind of filling (this super chocolate stuff called **ganache**), and even what font their names would be spelled out in. That place was the coolest. Maybe one day she could learn to make cakes like that.

Finally when it came, the baker and a helper brought it in to the big table in the center of the room. It had two **tiers,** was green and white, and had both of their names, one on each layer.

"What an awesome cake! I can't wait to eat it!" Sarah said, hardly **containing** her excitement.

"You'll have to wait," her mom said "The party isn't for another couple of hours."

"I know, but it just looks so good!" Sarah groaned.

"You can wait, just like everyone else." Her mom told her, giving her a look. Sarah sighed, took one last look at the cake, and went back to her crepe paper.

After what seemed like hours, but was really only another twenty minutes or so, the first few guests began to arrive. They were all decked out in their party finest. The girls were wearing their abayas, and summer hijabs. It was finally time to get the party started!

People started to pile presents onto a table in the corner. They "oooed" and "ahhed" at the cake, and hurried off towards the pool. Once plenty of splashing had been accomplished, the girls **clambered** out of the pool towards pizza and cake, much to Sarah's content.

All of her friends gathered around, eager as she was for the cake. Their mom started it by reciting Qur'aan.

What a wonderful way to spend one's Eid. Qura'aan, a party, and great food. "Alhamdullilah," said Sarah.

Narrated Anas bin Malik:

The Prophet *(Salallahu alayhi was salam)* never proceeded (for the prayer) on the Day of 'Id-ul-Fitr unless he had eaten some dates. Anas also narrated: The Prophet used to eat odd number of dates.

(Bukhari)

1. **Decorations:** something used to decorate or to make something else more beautiful.
2. **Ganache**
3. **Tiers:** a layer placed one on top of the other in a sequence.
4. **Containing:** controlling, restraining, holding back.
5. **Clambered:** climbing in an awkward way using hands and feet.

Helping Your Sibling

"Are you sure you are ok?" Sarah asked, checking in on her brother one more time.

"Yeah, I'll be ok," Sami said. He was a little paler than usual, and several **scrapes** and bruises were showing up on his face and arms. Earlier that day, Sami had been riding his bike, and had decided to try to go over a jump. He didn't aim his wheel in the right direction and when he hit  the jump he flipped his bike, landed on his leg, and the bike landed on top of him. He had tried to get up and quite **rapidly** discovered that his leg was broken.

After getting back from the hospital, "Sami was sore, bruised, and **exhausted**. All he wanted to do was sleep and forget about his accident. The longer he stayed in bed the **sorer** he felt and the less he wanted to deal with what had happened to him. Sarah, hoping to cheer him up, came in the next morning to do just that.

"Hey, bro," she said, peeking her head into his room. "How are you doing today?"

He groaned and rolled over, mumbling something about how she should leave him alone. She stepped into the room anyway, ignoring him.

"I was hoping we could hang out today, maybe play some games or something. That is if you are feeling up to it." Sarah said hopefully. All Sami did was stare at the wall. Sarah frowned. Sami was obviously upset about his leg being broken, but he didn't want to talk about it.

"If you want to play rummy or need something, I'll be around. I hope you feel better." Sarah said slowly leaving the room.

"It's just not fair," Sami said.

"What's not fair?" Sarah asked, turning back into the room.

"This horrible broken leg. I can't play baseball now. I'm going to be stuck inside for 6 weeks, doing nothing. It's just not fair!" Sami glowered, crossing his arms.

"Yeah, it is kind of rough. But you can make the best of it. I know there are books you want to read, and we can play games together. I don't think it will be quite as awful as you think it will be." She looked at him with a smile.

Sami looked at the floor. "Thanks. It's just hard for me. I'm not used to it. I appreciate your help. I just think that it will take time to get used to the whole thing. Sitting around isn't my thing, you know?" He looked sad and frustrated.

"I know it's going to be hard for you, but I'll be her for you. You don't have to deal with this all by yourself. You'll heal up and be back to baseball faster than you know it. So, how about that game of Qu'raan Challenge?" She asked, hoping he had been won over.

Sami looked down at his cast, then up at his sister. Taking a deep breath, he said "Yeah, I think playing that game would be great. Sign me up."

"Oh!" Sarah said. "Speaking of signing things, can I be the first person to sign your cast?"

Laughing, Sami said, "Of course you can!" and grabbed a marker from his bed side table.

Narrated Abu Musa:

The Prophet (*Salallahu alayhi was salam*) said, "Free the captives, feed the hungry and pay a visit to the sick."

(Bukhari)

---

1. **Scrapes:** scratches, an injury or damage from scraping.
2. **Rapidly:** quickly, speedily, hastily.
3. **Exhausted:** tired, worn out and shattered.
4. **Sorer:** painful, hurtful and annoyed.

The Remote Control

"It is my turn!" Sarah cried out, reaching for the remote.

"It is not, and this is my favorite show, you can wait!" Sami said, holding the remote up over her head and jumping up and down.

"I hate this show, and you know I do. You know I do, you are watching it just to make me mad!" Sarah shouted.

"I am not! Mom says you aren't allowed to call people names! I'm telling!" Sami called back at her mockingly.

Sarah stomped her foot. "But it is *my* turn! I've been waiting! You have had tons of turns, it's not fair that you get a turn just because this show is on!"

Sami put the remote under his arm. "I have not had bunches of turns. I get the same number you do! You are just mad that my turn gets to happen when 'Randy's **Renegade**' is on."

"Am not!" Sarah **retorted**, folding her arms.

"Are too! And if you don't quit it I'm totally calling mom in here." Sami stuck his tongue out at her.

"But it is *my* turn, dweeb! I want to watch 'Pony **Polonaise**"! Sarah stomped her foot.

"Mo-oom!" Sami shouted. "Sarah is calling me names!"

Their mom came into the room with a frown.

"Sarah, is this true?"

Sarah looked at the floor. She nodded. "Yes ma'am," She muttered.

"Well dear, you know the consequences for calling people names. You have to go to your room until dinner." Mom said, giving her 'the look'. Sami stood behind Mom and stuck his tongue out at her one more time. He then **triumphantly** went over to the couch and turned on the TV.

Sarah **sulkily** walked up the stairs, angry that her brother had told on her, frustrated that he had gotten to watch the television program that he had wanted to, and upset that she was trapped in her room until dinner. It just wasn't fair. He always got what he wanted. She sat down on her bed, frowning. Laying down, she fell asleep.

* * *

She woke up with a start hearing her mom call her. Wiping the sleep from her eyes, she slowly got up and went down to dinner. Sitting down across from her brother, she looked at the table. She wasn't angry anymore, but she didn't want him to keep sticking his tongue. She knew what she had done wasn't very kind, but she still didn't think it was fair that he kept rubbing it in. Dinner was a rather tedious affair at night, with Sarah trying to avoid looking at Sami, and Sami trying to get her to look at him.

After the dishes were cleared, Sami came over to her and tapped her on the arm. "I'm sorry you got in trouble. 'Pony Polonaise' is on again tonight, and I'll watch it with you." He said with a small smile.

"I'm sorry too. It wasn't very nice of me to call you names. You don't have to watch that show if you don't want to," Sarah said, with sad glance at her shoes.

Sami put his arm around her shoulder and said, "It would be my pleasure to watch it with you sis!" He walked her into the living room and plunked them both onto the couch and handed her the remote.

Allaah (Subhana wa Ta'la) says in the Qur'aan:

"Only those who are patient shall *receive* their reward in full, without reckoning. ... Truly, Allaah is with *As-Sabirun* (the patient)."

(The Qur'aan, Chapter 2:153)

---

1. **Renegade:** somebody who leaves a group, religion or cause to follow another.
2. **Retorted:** replied angrily and snapped.
3. **Polonaise:** a slow dance consisting of a stroll.
4. **Triumphantly:** having achieved a great success.
5. **Sulkily:** grumpily, crossly and moodily.

Every Day is Mother's Day!

Sarah was sitting in the living room playing with the cat when her mom came home. She looked sad and worn out. "What's wrong mom?" Sarah asked.

"Oh sweetie, I just had a rough day at work. I'll be ok. I think I'm just going to go up to my room for a little while." Mom said, taking her shoes off.

"If you need anything, let me know," Sarah called after her as she went up the stairs. Sarah frowned. It wasn't like her mom to come home from work looking so upset. She was usually happy and **bouncy**. It must have been a really bad day. Maybe there was something she could do for her. Something that would cheer her up.

Going into the kitchen, Sarah looked around, hoping for inspiration. Her mom really liked tea, but Sarah wasn't allowed to use the stove by herself. That idea was a no go. **Scanning** the room, she saw a vase in the cabinet. Flowers! Flowers would be perfect. They are colorful, they smell good, and they are just the thing that mom needed to cheer up.

Sarah went and fetched the step stool and carefully got the vase down from the cabinet. She put it gently down on the counter, and put the stool away. Now all she needed was the flowers. Luckily, there were beautiful flowers in the backyard. Her dad cut flowers to bring them into the house all the time. Digging through the drawer for a pair of scissors, Sarah began to envision the bouquet of flowers she would create. They had Black-eyed Susan's, Posies, Daisies, and a **plethora** of other flowers that she didn't even know the names of. She went into the backyard and carefully began to cut some flowers.

Getting all the flowers she needed, she went into the kitchen and laid them on the counter, just like her dad did. Filling the vase with some water, she put the flowers in the vase a few at a time until she thought it was perfect. Smiling at her work, she carefully picked up the vase and headed upstairs.

"Mom?" She said, knocking on the door.

"Yes dear?" Her mom said, sounding a little **strained**.

"I have something' for you. Can I come in? It will just be for a second." Sarah called through the door.

Hearing a word of **assent**, she carefully opened the door, being mindful of the flowers. "Hey Mom, I got went and got these for you. I hope you feel better." Sarah said, putting the flowers on the dresser.

Her mom looked surprised. "Aww, Sweetheart! Thank you so very much, those are just what I needed!" She said, sweeping Sarah up into a hug. "How very kind of you to think of me. I really needed that right now."

"Anything to make you smile Mom," Sarah said, and hugged her mom back, glad that she had been able to help.

Narrated Abu Huraira:

A man came to the Prophet (*Salallahu alayhi was salam*) and said, "O Allaah's Apostle! Who is more entitled to be treated with the best companionship by me?" The Prophet said, "Your mother." The man said. "Who is next?" The Prophet said, "Your mother." The man further said, "Who is next?" The Prophet said, "Your mother." The man asked for the fourth time, "Who is next?" The Prophet said, "Your father."

(Bukhari)

---

1. **Bouncy:** lively, bubbly, playful.
2. **Scanning:** to look over and around for something carefully.
3. **Plethora:** a very large amount of something.
4. **Strained:** worried, stressed and tensed.
5. **Assent:** agreement, consent, acceptance.

Live in The Moment!

It was a steamy hot Wednesday in June. Everyone was dying for school to just be over, and Sarah could tell that her teacher was getting **exasperated**. No one was **alert**, and it just seemed like there was nothing she could do to get anyone to **concentrate**. There was a boy in the back making paper airplanes, another was half asleep. Some of the girls were giggling about something one of the older kids did outside. Everyone wanted it to be summer vacation, including her teacher.

"Ok, guys, we have to get this assignment done today," Her teacher said, looking out at all of them.

A few kids groaned, and some of them put their heads on their desks. "Look, I know it is hot and uncomfortable in here, but we have to do the best we can. I need you all to put on your best listening ears and stick it out just a little bit longer." A paper airplane flew through the air and landed on her desk. The group of girls giggled some more.

Ms. Muhammad **crumpled** up the plane and threw it in the trash. She gave a look out to the boys in the back that said 'this isn't the time for this', and grabbed a stack of worksheets off of her desk. They slowly made their way down the rows, and when Sarah got hers and looked at, she almost groaned. It was another math worksheet. She didn't hate math, but this was not the time to do it. Her brain felt like a melting popsicle.

"So, class, let's get to business," Ms Muhammad

said, and began the lesson.

It was all Sarah could to not stare out the window like the giggly girls in the front corner, or even start making her own paper air planes. She kept telling herself that math was important, for some reason.

"Ok, Sarah, what is the answer to 5?" Ms. Muhammad asked, looking at her **pointedly**.

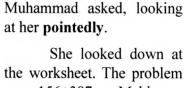

She looked down at the worksheet. The problem was 156+397=_ Making a few **scribbles** on her paper she looked up and said "553?"

"Good job, Sarah! Thank you for paying attention." Ms Muhammad smiled and continued to the next student with less success.

Glad she had been listening and paying attention, Sarah sat back in her seat. It could be summer after class was over. Until then, she still had to be a student.

Narrated by 'Abdullah bin 'Umar :

The Talbiya of the Prophet (*Salallahu alayhi was salam*) was : 'Labbaika Allahumma labbaik, Labbaika la sharika Laka labbaik, Inna-l-hamda wan-ni'mata Laka walmu Lk, La sharika Laka' (I respond to Your call O Allah, I respond to Your call, and I am obedient to Your orders, You have no partner, I respond to Your call All the praises and blessings are for You, All the sovereignty is for You, And You have no partners with you.

(Bukhari)

---

1. **Exasperated:** angry, frustrated, and annoyed.
2. **Alert:** aware, awake, ready, watchful, keen.
3. **Concentrate:** focus, think give attention to.
4. **Crumpled:** to press or crush and cause wrinkles.
5. **Pointedly**: in a deliberate, careful or purposeful way.
6. **Scribbles:** doodles, writing quickly or hastily.

Being Smart with your Money

"You guys have just got to see these!" Amira said, almost fit to burst. She **plunked** herself down on the carpet in the coat room, and pulled a very colorful package of cards out of her book bag. "These cards are just the best! They are the Mandy's World trading cards. You collect all of the different accessories, cities, and Mindy and her friends for the game. It is great!" She spurted out in one breath.

"Sure, they are cool if you are into Mandy's Word. It doesn't really matter to me because my mom says they are a waste of money. " Nadia said **matter-of-factually**.

"A waste of money?" gasped Amira. "You're kidding me right? This game is so much fun! My sister and I played it all last night. You don't know what you are talking about. It is worth every penny."

"If you say so," said Leena, shrugging. "I'd rather get some new books, or a new abaya. You have to buy at least ten packages to make the game any fun, and I don't want to spend my allowance on that."

"Well, I didn't have to spend my allowance on them. I used Eid money from my grandmother. I only need twenty more dollars to get the rest of the packs I am missing. I think I can **convince** my mom to give me the money." She said, **smirking**.

"That seems kind of greedy. Do you really need the rest of them? Between you and your sister don't you have 10 packs of cards?" Sarah asked.

"Well, I mean, between the two of us we have all the cards, but I want all of them myself. My sister totally isn't going to share." Amira said.

"How do you know that she isn't going to share? Have you asked?" Leena asked her.

"No, of course I haven't asked her," Amira said **sullenly**. "I just want my own!" Amira was upset that no one wanted to share in the joy of her card game. It seemed like they were all ganging up against her. "There isn't anything wrong with wanting more things!"

"No, having things isn't a bad, but wanting a lot of things you don't need isn't good. There are people that don't even have anything, and they would be grateful for just a few of the things that we have." Sarah said.

Amira looked over at Sarah a little puzzled. "I guess I never thought about it like that. I mean, I do have a lot of toys and games already," she said, as if she was thinking about the things she owned. "You guys are right; I don't *really* need all of the packs. I'll ask my sister. I'm sure she will share sometimes. We can work something out, I'm sure of it."

"That's great! I'm sure you can too. Maybe you can save your money up for something important." Nadia said. Leena and Sarah nodded.

"Sometimes when you have a lot of things, I guess it is hard to think about the things you really need," Amira said. "Thanks guys. I'll try and be less greedy from now on!"

Narrated by Abu Huraira:

A man asked the Prophet (*Salallahu alayhi was salam*, "O Allaah's Apostle! What kind of charity is the best?" He replied. "To give in charity when you are healthy and greedy hoping to be wealthy and afraid of becoming poor. Don't delay giving in charity till the time when you are on the death bed when you say, 'Give so much to so-and-so and so much to so-and so,' and at that time the property is not yours but it belongs to so-and-so (i.e. your inheritors)."

(Bukhari)

1. **Plunked:** placed, pushed, dropped, put.
2. **Matter-of-factually:** in fact, actually,
3. **Smirking:** grinning, to smile in a self-satisfied way.

My New Earrings

"Hey you guys! Did you see my new earrings! My mom got them for me. Aren't they awesome?" Nadia said, **bounding** into the classroom. They were little silver studs that sparkled in the sunlight.

"Yeah, those are really nice. Where did she get them?" Leena asked.

"Oh, we went jewelry shopping at the mall yesterday. It was so cool. She got me five other pairs too!" she replied, tilting her head back and forth to show them off.

"I wish I had earrings like that," Leena said. "My mom won't even let me get my ears pierced until I am 12."

"Wow, really? That's super lame. I got mine **pierced** last year. It wasn't too bad. They spray your ears with this stuff that makes them super cold, then they pierce them. It hardly even hurts." Nadia said, very proud of her earrings.

"My mom said I'm not old enough to get mine pierced either." Sarah said. "I have to wait until I'm 10."

"I wish we didn't have to wait," Leena said. "I'm so jealous!"

Sarah shrugged. "I guess our moms have a good reason for not wanting us to get our ears pierced."

"What kind of reason?" Leena asked rather

disgruntled. "I'm going to be the very last girl in our grade to get my ears pierced!"

"I don't know, maybe our mothers don't think we are old enough to take care of piercing. I know you have to clean them a lot, and make sure it doesn't get **infected**."

"Eww, they can get infected?" Leena asked, making a face.

"Sure they can. You are having a piece of metal shot into your ear." Nadia said knowingly. "I was given a speech on how careful you have to be when you first get them pierced. They give you cleaner that you have to use everyday, and you have to twist them all the time to keep the hole open. It kind of was a lot of work."

"Maybe my mom knows what she is talking about." Leena said. "I don't think I want to do all that stuff right now. I think I would forget."

"Yeah, my mom had to remind me a lot. Maybe it would have been better to wait until I was older. Well it's done and over with now. "

"And We have enjoined on man (to be dutiful and good) to his parents. His mother bore him in weakness and hardship upon weakness and hardship, and his weaning is in two years - give thanks to Me and to your parents. Unto Me is the final destination."

(The Qur'aan, Chapter #31, Verse #14)

---

1. **Bounding:** jumping, bouncing, hopping.
2. **Pierced:** to make a hole in something.
3. **Disgruntled:** annoyed. irritated, displeased.
4. **Infected:** to spread germs or disease to.

Have you bought "SuperCharge Homeschooling's Pre-K & Kindergarten Curriculum"

Pre-K Curriculum

Kindergarten Curriculum

Have You Bought The Series: "Things Every Kid Should Know: Drugs, Alcohol, Smoking, Bullying and Junk Food" for Your Kids By An "10 Year Old" Author, Alya Nuri?

Have You Bought The Series: "Things Every Kid Should Know: Strangers and Fire" for Your Kids By A "7 Year Old" Author, Zafar Nuri?

Have You Bought The Series: "Things Every Kid Should Know: Hand Washing" for Your Kids By A "6 Year Old" Author, Arsalon Nuri?

Books By Zohra Sarwari

E-books by Zohra Sarwari